9113000020122

D0715096

BRENT LIBRARIES
Please return/renew this item
by the last date shown.
Books may also be renewed by
phone or online.
Tel: 0115 929 3388
On-line **www.brent.gov.uk/libraryservice**

Look out for other exciting stories
in the *Shades* series:

COMING IN TO LAND

Dennis Hamley

Evans

Published by Evans Brothers Limited
2A Portman Mansions
Chiltern St
London W1U 6NR

© Dennis Hamley 2009

First published in 2009

British Library Cataloguing in Publication Data
  Hamley, Dennis.
    Coming in to land. -- (Shades)
    1. Young adult fiction.
    I. Title II. Series
    823.9'14-dc22

  ISBN-13: 9780237539498

Editor: Julia Moffatt
Designer: Rob Walster

Contents

Chapter One

First Flight

Jack didn't expect it like this. The winch far below dragged the steel hawser upwards and the tiny two-seater training glider juddered and shook so much that it seemed its nose section must be wrenched off. The voice of Flying Officer O'Brian, the instructor, sounded from behind him in the open cockpit.

'When we've reached a thousand feet I'll pull the cable-release and shout "Let go". You'll be doing this next time so you'll shout the same now when I do so I know you've got it right. OK?'

'OK,' Jack answered.

Another few seconds of juddering, then: 'Let go,' came the shout, Jack repeated it and suddenly felt free, floating on a waterless sea, silent but for the rush of air of the wind on his face, perfect peace, *magic*. He looked down at patchwork fields, green, brown, yellow, roads stretching grey across them, cars and lorries like tiny toys. He saw the grass airfield with the other training glider on the ground, winches like tiny prehistoric monsters at the perimeter fence, the windsock hanging limp on this still, hot day. Glorious.

Sudden fright. Up so high in a tiny box with creaking wings and no engine, a frail little thing at the mercy of every breath of air – if he looked sideways he saw the wingtips shake as if to snap off. So fragile, surely they'd break up in mid-air…

O'Brian's voice again.

'No daydreaming. Put your hands on the joystick. It's dual-control so don't grasp it tight, you must feel how I use it. Keep your feet on the rudder bars. Don't push on them. You've got three dials in front of you. One's the airspeed indicator and when we're up here we keep it about thirty knots straight and level. You sure won't like it if we get too slow and stall. The next dial tells you the height, the third whether we've got lift.' Silence. 'When do we get lift, Rayner?'

'When we find a thermal,' said Jack.

'Good. And what's a thermal? And don't say your underpants.'

'Warm air rising.'

'And is today good for thermals?'

'Yes. It's hot, no wind and we're over fields. Cornfields are best.'

'Well, at least you listened to what we told you.'

This first flight lasted twenty minutes. In that time Jack was shown turning, banking and getting out of a stall.

'You'll do this yourself in a few days,' said O'Brian.

It didn't seem possible, but Jack felt a thrill of joy just the same. They hit a thermal and rose to fifteen hundred feet. When O'Brian said, 'Sorry, Rayner, but it's time to go home,' he was really regretful.

'Now for landing,' said O'Brian.

Landing. Landing was difficult. Jack
knew it was the most dangerous part of
any flight.

The year was 1943, the bombing war was
at its height and Jack had heard of bombers
crashing on landing. Lancasters and
American Flying Fortresses which had been
shot up by German fighters would toil
home across the sea to their airfields and
then, when the hard work had been done,
plough into the ground at the very end of
their missions.

But at least they had engines to throttle
back to help them slow down: the little
glider had nothing but a rushing wind and
a boy at the controls.

'We land anywhere inside that square
marked out on the grass,' said O'Brian.
Jack looked down. It looked the size of his
thumbnail. It *was* impossible.

O'Brian lined the glider up so they would come over the winches towards the magic square.

'Shallow dive,' he said. 'Check height, check rudder, wing tips level with horizon, ease stick forward just a little.'

Jack felt the joystick move forward slightly and the nose drop. He saw the green below come up to meet them, their speed increased, the wind rushed past with a swooshing noise and now the square was wider.

But surely they were coming in too steeply? Jack drew his breath in panic. They were going to hit the ground nose first.

Then O'Brian said in his matter-of-fact voice, 'Watch this, Rayner and watch well. I ease the stick back and level out the instant the airfield stops looking like a green tablecloth and I can pick out individual blades of grass and then I say

"Check". Got that?'

Jack gulped.

'Yes,' he muttered.

The ground was meeting them very fast.
He didn't believe O'Brian, there wouldn't
be time to pull out, it couldn't happen,
they'd plough into—

'Check!' O'Brian shouted and the little
plane was suddenly level and skimming
easily over the ground until it gently
kissed the grass, came to a halt and canted
over so the starboard wingtip rested on
the ground.

'How was that, Rayner?' he said.

'Fantastic,' Jack replied.

'Wait till you're on your own. Then you'll
know how fantastic it is.' O'Brian smiled.
'Get unbuckled and see what your mates
thought of it.'

But when he walked across and joined

them where they sat on the ground waiting for their flights, Cecil Pirbright was the only one who spoke.

'Pity,' he said. 'You came back.'

Chapter Two
Chances

The Second World War had dragged on for nearly four years. Great battles had raged in Russia, North Africa and across the Pacific Ocean. Every night from all over eastern England, the Lancasters and Halifaxes of RAF Bomber Command took off and bombed German cities, and every day American Flying Fortresses aimed for German factories

The war had hit the cadets of Crumpton Air Training Corps as much as anybody else. Jack's father was with the Eighth Army in Africa, even now preparing to invade Sicily and Italy. The fathers of some boys had been killed or wounded. Cecil Pirbright's elder brother was training to fly *real* planes. Like everybody else, the boys had thrilled to the exploits of the fighter pilots in the Battle of Britain and now they followed the missions of the bomber crews with equal enthusiasm.

A thousand bomber raids on Berlin, bombing the dams – there wasn't a single cadet who didn't long to be up there with them.

Now was their chance. Someone high up in the RAF had thought that gliding lessons for cadets would be a good way of spotting potential pilots for later in the war, if it lasted that long.

So now they were at the little grass airfield at Torwood for a week's preliminary gliding course to see if any of them ever might be. A week when they could forget ration books because the RAF was feeding them.

There were fifteen cadets sharing two training gliders. They had four instructors, all RAF pilots recovering from injuries and sent on training duties before flying again. Jack was fourteen, old enough to go gliding by a mere few days.

He had joined the ATC without telling his mother.

When he recalled the look of sheer shock on her face when he turned up at home in what looked like full RAF uniform he didn't know whether to laugh or feel guilty.

When he said he wanted to go on the gliding camp he thought she'd go up the wall with fury. Instead, she asked when and when he told her she said, 'Actually it would suit me very well. Joy's in hospital for more tests that week and I want to stay there with her.'

His sister Joy was nine and often going into hospital. Well, of course he was sorry about Joy, but she'd saved him a lot of trouble.

All the other cadets were older and bigger. Some he didn't like, Cecil Pirbright for example, the oldest there and squadron sergeant as well.

He was big, running to fat if he wasn't careful – Jack wondered how a little glider could get airborne with him wedged in it. Pirbright's braying voice made Jack's teeth grate. He never stopped talking about his brother and how he was going to do even better.

He seemed to think that his sergeant's stripes would make him God's gift to the RAF, certain to fly the latest planes and end up a wing commander at least. Anyone could tell it was his greatest ambition – no, more than that, his obsession. He hunted in a pack with his cronies: Spinks, whose father was in the Navy, and Fordyce, whose father was in a reserved occupation so didn't have to join up.

He had conned Flight Lieutenant Chapman – really just a teacher in a uniform and too old to be called up – into promoting his two mates to corporal. Jack knew they thought he was too young to be on the camp and he didn't like it.

If they found one chink in his armour

they'd probe and worry at it until his life was a misery. They had rank and weren't afraid to use their stripes to throw their weight around. The rest knew them too well to bother. Jack had a nasty feeling he'd be picked on.

Pirbright started early.

'If I had my way you wouldn't be here. Kids your age shouldn't be allowed. I'm seventeen, I can drive a car already and if only we could get some petrol I'd be doing it all the time. I bet you can hardly ride a bike.'

'Yes I can,' Jack answered indignantly, but Pirbright wasn't listening, which was no surprise because he never did.

They were flying in reverse alphabetical order so Pirbright was next.

'Now see how it should be done,' he said as O'Brian called him over.

Jack watched as the winches started up, O'Brian shouted, 'Take up slack,' the plane rose, and the towing hook was released a thousand feet up and fell lazily to the ground.

Jack imagined Pirbright in the pilot's seat trying to look like a Battle of Britain ace. He strained his eyes to keep them in sight but they were going too far afield.

Half an hour passed before Jack saw the glider's descent, straight and true, and the perfect, gentle landing. Pirbright's flight had been twice as long as the others had.

Jack watched him unbuckle and get out. O'Brian climbed out as well and said something. Pirbright laughed. O'Brian laughed too and touched him companionably on the shoulder.

They seemed like equals, two survivors of a dangerous mission landing together.

Pirbright was smiling triumphantly. 'See that landing?' he said. 'That was me at the controls, not him. He says I'm a natural and I could go solo straight away without all this right- and left-hand circuit rubbish. I'll be on Spitfires before I'm twenty. I just hope the war lasts long enough.'

'What's it like up there, Cec?' said Spinks.

'You'll soon find out,' said Pirbright. 'It's your turn next.'

'I bet I won't be as good as you,' said Spinks.

'No,' said Pirbright. 'No, you won't.'

Chapter Three

Disaster

The first night in the corrugated-iron
Nissen hut passed quietly. The windows
were blacked out, as they were everywhere
else while the war was on. The airfield
stretched dark and quiet beyond them.
There was no night flying from this isolated
spot. In the guardroom and round the

perimeter track, armed sentries took turns keeping silent watch.

Inside the hut Jack made sure he took a bed as far away from Pirbright as he could. Ronnie Peabody was in the next bed: not one of Jack's best friends but all right.

'How did you get on?' Jack asked him.

'OK, I suppose,' said Ronnie.

'It's great, isn't it, flying gliders.'

'Not bad,' said Ronnie.

This wasn't getting very far so Jack turned over and went to sleep, to dream of wonderful flights and disastrous landings.

Next day Jack made two more circuits. After the second he felt quite a veteran. Winching up, letting go, feeling free like a bird, now seemed so natural. O'Brian let him take the controls and he soon felt used to them.

On this limpid blue day there were plenty of thermals to chase and when they found one Jack felt the little plane lift as if the palm of a giant's hand was pushing them up from underneath.

But each time they lined up for the approach and saw the tiny thumbnail of grass to land in, he shivered. He knew he'd never manage it, but smash straight into the hard ground.

'Watch and learn,' said O'Brian. 'Feel what I do and when I do it. Get it stuck in your head, because next time up you'll do it yourself.'

O'Brian made the landing seem natural and easy. Jack didn't get out but stayed buckled up in the cockpit thinking about the impossibility of it all until O'Brian said, 'Stir yourself, Rayner. Others want to fly as much as you.'

Pirbright was next. When he landed he smirked and said, 'I'm going solo tomorrow. O'Brian says it will be a record, the shortest time to solo ever known here. Not even my brother could have done that. He's on advanced trainers already and he's only three years older than me.'

'Good on you, Cec,' said Spinks.

'You'll do it easy,' said Fordyce.

Pirbright smirked again, as if to say, 'Of course. But you won't because you're all losers.'

When everyone had had two flights the instructors decided there was time for a third, easy enough with two planes.

When Jack's turn came O'Brian said, 'You land. You've got to do it sooner or later and now's as good a time as any.'

This time Jack hated every moment of

the flight. He'd forgotten everything he'd done yesterday and O'Brian kept having to take over.

'Don't worry so much,' he said. 'You can do it.'

He pulled himself together and got out of a practice stall, which made him feel better.

'Right, let's go home now,' said O'Brian. 'There's no wind to worry about. If you can't land now, you never will.'

I suppose you think that will encourage me, thought Jack. *I feel worse.*

He lined up for the final approach. They passed over the road next to the airfield. A bus travelled just below them and he saw passengers staring upwards, pointing him out to each other. The winches seemed nearer than they should be.

'Take her down yourself,' said O'Brian.

'We're too low,' said Jack.

'Don't worry. You're doing all right.'

But he did worry. *My descent's too shallow. I'm too high.* Cold fear rose in him.

'Fine so far,' said O'Brian. 'Remember, ease the stick back when you can pick out the blades of grass and shout "check". I'll shout "check" myself if I think you're too late.

I'll overshoot. He saw the cadets watching, impatient for their turn. *I've got to steepen this a bit.* He eased the stick ever so slightly forward.

'Careful,' he heard O'Brian say.

The green carpet was rushing up to meet him. Then he had an awful doubt. What did O'Brian mean about the grass? Should he check when it stopped looking like a snooker table, or wait until he could see literally every blade of grass, count buttercups and daisies, see where Cecil Pirbright's huge feet had flattened them?

He was still trying to work it out when O'Brian screamed, 'Check for pity's sake, you silly little twerp!'

The glider's nose ploughed into the ground with a shuddering shock and the crack of breaking spars. For a second he blacked out.

When he came round his head was spinning. There was complete silence, complete stillness. He thought: *Is this what Heaven's like?*

'Are you all right, Rayner?' said O'Brian.

'I think so,' said Jack.

'Unbuckle and try to get out.'

No limbs broken. His head was still spinning and he ached everywhere. He slipped his harness and struggled out. He tried to stand up but dizziness made him sit down again quickly. His nose began to bleed.

O'Brian was already out, seemingly none the worse for wear, looking at the ruined glider with the crumpled nose and snapped port wing and absently kicking a little hole in the ground with the toecap of his shoe.

Then he said, 'Well, it wasn't entirely your fault, Rayner. I should have taken over earlier. I thought you were ready for this but it looks like I was wrong.'

Jack, too busy staunching blood pouring from his nose, didn't answer.

'If right was right, you'd go straight up again because if you don't you'd never fly again. But you're in no fit state and besides, I reckon your mates would lynch you. Squeeze your nose with your handkerchief, get back to the hut and have a lie down.'

The others were approaching fast, Pirbright leading, and they did not look happy. Pirbright stood over him, arms folded, looking down.

'You stupid, idiotic little pillock,' he said.

'I couldn't help it,' Jack muttered.

'I know. That's why it's so sad. They let you on this course and now you've ruined it. Only one plane left between the lot of us. If I don't go solo tomorrow I'm going to kill you, Rayner.'

An RAF low-loader was crossing the grass and soon the little glider was lifted on the back.

O'Brian said, 'Back to normal service. Spinks, you're next.'

After Spinks had come down, only Turnbull and Williams were left, so the circuits were hardly delayed.

When they were finished, O'Brian said,

'We might not get an evening as still as this again. It's a pity to pack it in so early.'

He looked round the group.

'Pirbright?' he said. 'How about going solo now?'

'*Yeeaah!*' shouted Pirbright and punched the air with his fist.

'Listen up, the lot of you,' said O'Brian. 'I'll explain what our friend here will be doing because it will come to you all sooner or later. To qualify for your first solo license you do three circuits, one right-hand, one left-hand, one whichever way you like. Got that?'

'Yes, sir,' they chorused.

'Good. Now you're lucky, you're getting a demonstration from the most promising character in a glider that I've seen for many a long day and that's why he's going solo a week early.'

'Good luck, Cec,' said Fordyce and the rest raggedly repeated, 'Yes, good luck, Cec.'

'I don't need luck,' said Pirbright.

He was right. He did the three circuits with ease as the instructors stood in a little group and nodded wisely.

When he landed for the third and last time he unbuckled his harness, climbed out and actually said, 'Piece of cake,' as if the glider had changed into a Spitfire and he'd shot down three Messerschmitt 109s.

Then he strode over towards the hut, a colossus with admiring little henchmen, the *Queen Mary* surrounded by tugboats. Only Jack held back.

Chapter Four
Pirbright's Revenge

After they'd eaten in the airmen's mess, watched by curious erks in RAF blue uniforms, they played football on the grass outside until it was too dark to see, then they went into the hut.

Some played board games, others read. Pirbright didn't say much, even to Spinks and Fordyce. He lay on his bed, arms behind his head, thinking.

At last he said to Fordyce, 'Tell everyone to stop what they're doing. I want to say a few words.'

When he had quiet, Pirbright said, 'You saw what happened today.'

'Yeah,' said Spinks. 'You were brilliant, Cec.'

'I'm not talking about that. I mean about our little friend here, the one who's ruined the course for you.'

'And for you, Cec,' someone said.

'No, not for me,' said Pirbright. 'I've got what I came for. I'm beyond this place, these instructors, these pathetic little stringbag gliders. I'm destined for bigger things, like my brother. I'm only thinking about you. I'm thinking how unfair it is that one sad little runt who shouldn't be near this place, shouldn't have been allowed in a glider, shouldn't come within ten miles of anything that flies even if he's only a passenger, has wrecked everything. He deserves punishment. What do you think?'

'Whatever you say, Cec,' said Ronnie.

You traitor, thought Jack.

'It's not for me to say,' said Pirbright. 'It's your course now. Make it something that he won't forget in a hurry.'

'Well, we could tell Chapman back at school what we think,' said Fordyce.

'That useless cretin? Don't waste my time,' said Pirbright and Fordyce muttered,

'Sorry, Cec.'

'We could go to O'Brian,' said Spinks.

'You're a hopeless lot,' said Pirbright. 'It's always someone else who's got to do it, isn't it? You've got to do it yourselves. Just try and be a bit clever for a change.'

'Let's rough him up a bit,' said Ronnie, and now Jack thought,

You're a Judas, Ronnie.

'Have sense,' said Pirbright. 'You should—'

His voice tailed off and there was silence.

'Well, you suggest something then, Cec,' said Spinks at last.

Another silence.

'Cec?' said Spinks. 'Are you all right?'

Pirbright was sitting on the bed, his eyes fixed, glazed, vacant. A line of spittle dribbled down his chin.

Jack leant over and waved his hand in front of Pirbright's open eyes. Not even a blink.

'There's something wrong,' he said.

'You know it all, don't you?' said Spinks. 'Shut your face, you little twerp. He's thinking, that's all.'

'—do something for yourselves, nothing to do with O'Brian and Chapman, and something which won't go any further than between us. Our business and nobody else's. Right?'

Pirbright finished the sentence as if there had been no gap in between. Jack felt the gasp of relief in the room. Even so, no one came up with a suggestion.

'Well,' said Pirbright. 'While you morons have been staring at each other I've come up with a plan and it's to do with me, not you. Jack and me, we're going flying together.'

What does he mean? That's impossible, thought Jack.

The others thought the same.

'What do you mean, Cec?' said Fordyce.

'I mean,' said Pirbright slowly, as if

talking to toddlers, 'that I shall be taking him up tomorrow, not one of the instructors.'

'They'd never let you,' said Ronnie.

'They won't stop me. By the time they find out it'll be too late.'

'You're not allowed. You have to be a qualified pilot,' said Spinks.

'I've flown solo. O'Brian says I'm as good as some who've been flying for years. He'll be pleased, he'll say, "Good lad, I knew you'd do it".'

'You think you're brilliant, don't you?' Jack said daringly.

'Don't talk until you're asked to,' said Pirbright. 'That's settled then.'

'What if I won't go?' said Jack.

'You'll go. You've got no choice. If you breathe a word about it we'll say we don't know what you're talking about. When it's over we'll say you pestered me until I took you up for the sake of a quiet life.'

'Why would I want to go with you?' said Jack.

'Because you know you're useless and you're afraid of O'Brian so you want me to give you good advice and some flying time with no pressure. I'm only doing it for you.'

Whichever way Jack looked at it, he was trapped.

'And after we've landed, you'll be such a quivering wreck that you'll keep your feet planted on the ground for the rest of your life,' said Pirbright.

All night, Jack lay awake trying to find some way out. When his watch said half past three he remembered that Pirbright hadn't said how he would to manage the flight without the instructors knowing.

Then he felt happy. There was no way it could happen. Safe in the knowledge, he slept.

When he woke, his first thought was of Pirbright sitting silent on his bed, mouth open, eyes glazed over. He felt a little shiver of unease. He knew something was wrong because he'd seen it before.

Before breakfast, Pirbright said, 'I expect you slept quite well when you thought there was no way we could get winched up without anyone knowing.'

Jack would rather die than say yes.

'I've got bad news for you. I've got it all worked out. There's no escape, Rayner. I've got you just where I want you. And this is not just for me, it's for everyone in the squadron.'

He turned to the others.

'Isn't that so?' he said.

Spinks sniggered.

'Too right, Cec,' he said.

Pirbright turned back to Jack.

'I'm your sergeant and you can't disobey my orders,' he said. 'You've had it, Rayner.'

Chapter Five
Torment and Triumph

Jack's great hope was that he'd fly with O'Brian early and this time land perfectly. That would be one in the eye for Pirbright. But on this morning the flying went alphabetically, Abrams first. With only one plane, he'd be waiting the whole day.

The drill for each flight was that the

cadets got in, strapped themselves in the cockpit, checked the controls – rudder and ailerons – then called, 'Take up slack.'

An instructor on the ground signalled with his arm to let the winch operator know when to start winching, the cable tautened, the glider began to move and the pilot yelled, 'All out!'

Then the winch roared louder and the little plane bumped fast across the grass until it took off. Ronnie Peabody was the last to fly before, at Pirbright's suggestion which the instructors gladly agreed with, they broke for lunch.

An RAF Land Rover drove over, bringing sandwiches for the boys and taking the instructors to the officers' mess for lunch.

Jack had been surprised at this at first, but O'Brian made it clear that Pirbright was left responsible because he had the rank. It was a matter of trust.

'Right,' said Pirbright to Spinks. 'What did I tell you to do next?'

'Signal to the winch,' said Spinks.

'Good,' said Pirbright. He turned to Jack. 'Get in,' he said.

'No,' said Jack.

'I say *get in*, and so does everyone else.'

They surrounded him and moved in threateningly.

'Last time, Rayner,' said Pirbright. 'Or O'Brian won't see the marks on your body.'

Jack didn't believe him but there was a nasty threat underlying the words, so he scrambled into the front cockpit and buckled up.

Pirbright did the checks, then shouted, 'Take up slack.'

Spinks raised his arm to signal to

the winches.

'All out,' shouted Pirbright.

The glider moved. The winch operators hadn't suspected anything.

Juddering, noisy, the hook underneath pulling so hard that Jack thought it would wrench the nose off, they reached a thousand feet.

He wondered whether to shout, 'Let go,' and pull the handle himself. While he dithered, Pirbright did it.

'Ever thought what it's like to be trapped?' Pirbright called. 'Your fate lies in my hands. For all you know the reason I'm up here is because I just can't go on and this is a spectacular way to end it all. They'd talk about us for years. Fame at last. You'd like that, wouldn't you?'

'*Shut up, shut up, shut up*,' Jack screamed.

Pirbright laughed. 'Don't worry your

little head, Rayner. It's not likely that I'm a madman, is it? They won't let madmen fly Lancasters.'

For a moment Jack breathed easier.

'Still, perhaps I am. You never know.'

For a while they flew straight and level. Jack tried to enjoy the perfect blue sky, the green, brown and gold patchwork of fields below, the roads criss-crossing them.

Then Pirbright said, 'Ever wondered what it's like to loop the loop?'

Jack didn't answer.

'I'll take that as a yes. Let's try it, shall we?'

Suddenly they slipped downwards like a canoe sliding over a waterfall. The wind rose to a rushing roar, their speed gathered and they hurtled downwards out of control. Surely they'd plough into the ground and make a crater, with them at the bottom.

Jack closed his eyes in pure terror, then opened them, fascinated. The ground came up too fast. He saw each ridge and furrow of a ploughed field like a close-up photograph. Violent death was a split second away.

At the last instant Pirbright yanked the stick back. Jack felt the fuselage buckle and the spars groan. The wings would fall off, they'd break up in mid-air.

The G forces as the sheer impetus of the dive made them climb again forced him back in his seat. For an instant he blacked out.

When he came to, the plane was intact but upside down and only righted itself as Pirbright pushed it into another dive.

The same scare, the same G forces, the same leaving behind of his stomach, but this time at the top of the climb out of the dive, Jack thought: *he can really do this. He is a natural. So he can't scare me any more.*

Then they flew straight and level for a few minutes. Suddenly Pirbright pulled the stick up so the nose lifted. Jack's stomach turned over yet again.

He knew Pirbright was deliberately putting the glider into a stall which would only be righted when they'd almost fallen out of the sky.

I'll show him, thought Jack.

He pushed the stick forward: the glider regained speed and flew level again.

'Clever,' said Pirbright. 'Let's see what you can do with this.'

Another stall. But before Jack could push the stick down the glider canted sickeningly over to the left and began to spiral helplessly.

'You've put us in a spin,' he screamed.

Pirbright laughed.

'I know,' he replied. 'And I'm not sure how to get out of it. Now let me think… I'm sure I read about it somewhere.'

Just as real terror was returning, Jack felt the plane right itself again.

'I remembered just in time,' said Pirbright. 'Aren't you the lucky one?'

Jack was trembling. He wanted to be down, go home, never come to this dreadful place again.

'You've won, Pirbright,' he muttered, though not loud enough to be heard.

'I'm bored,' said Pirbright. 'Let's go back. Haven't we had a lovely time up here?'

They were nearing the airfield. Soon Pirbright would make his approach.

Jack sat dead still, wondering what final torture he'd be put through. He heard a thud behind him.

What's he doing now? he thought.

Then another, and another: a series of sharp, irregular noises. Then what sounded like a groan. Jack risked a look over his shoulder.

Pirbright lolled back into his seat, his head at a strange angle. His eyes were open and staring, like last night. His arms jerked. There was spittle on his face.

Jack was only fearful for a second. He knew what he was seeing. What a fool he was not to realise last night. Pirbright was having a fit.

He'd seen enough all these years with Joy. That's why she was in hospital for more tests. But the doctors were certain now. His sister suffered from epilepsy and had fits just like this. And now he knew Pirbright was an epileptic too.

But that meant Pirbright couldn't fly the

glider. For the moment it was flying itself, but that wouldn't last for long and soon it would stall naturally. Then they'd just drop out of the sky, Jack, Pirbright, glider and all, and that would be the end of them.

Everything depended on Jack: keeping straight and level and then – Jack gulped – *landing on his own.* So he'd better screw up his courage and get on with it, otherwise he wouldn't be on this earth for very much longer.

He grasped the stick, pushed it forward slightly to keep up his airspeed and started to make his approach.

Now, into the wind: the windsock below shows which direction. Line up to the landing area. Wingtips level, grasp the stick lightly, forward, easy, easy, don't rush it, keep an eye on the speedo and altimeter, watch the ground ahead, easy, easy, carefully, carefully, keep it straight, don't let the glider slip either way, keep that little landing square in focus, nothing else matters.

Ignore the thuds and the groaning behind you, watch the grass, approach speed not too fast, not too slow, here comes the grass, green expanse like a snooker table, nearer, nearer – and suddenly it's individual blades of grass, I can see them, now I know what O'Brian meant, ease the stick back, gently, gently, I feel the skid kiss the grass, I'm here, so smoothly, so perfectly, and now I'm safe on the ground and I unbuckle the straps, jump out and shout, 'Help me!'

Nobody came.

'Help me!' Jack screamed again. 'He's ill.'

He leaned over Pirbright and gently undid the buckle. He put his arms behind his shoulders and tried to ease him out. This had to be done quickly but so very,

very gently. The cadets stood some way off, frightened.

'Someone come, for pity's sake,' Jack yelled.

At last Ronnie Peabody warily approached.

'I'll take his shoulders, you take his knees,' Jack told him. 'We'll get him out of the cockpit and then lay him on the ground. For heaven's sake be careful, he could swallow his tongue if we're rough with him. Watch his arms and legs, he could hit you, he doesn't mean it, he doesn't know he's doing it.'

Somehow they managed it, the two of them.

'Put him on his side,' said Jack and when they had done it, they drew Pirbright's legs up so he was lying as if in bed.

'They call that the foetal position,'

said Jack.

'How do you know?' said Ronnie.

'I've had practice,' Jack replied.

Pirbright was quiet now. He was regaining consciousness.

After a moment or two he sat up, blinked and said, 'I feel terrible.' Then, 'What am I doing down here?'

'You had a fit,' said Jack.

'Don't talk rubbish,' said Pirbright.

'Sorry, but you did,' said Jack. 'Have you had fits before?'

Pirbright didn't answer.

The others now dared to come across, sheepish and embarrassed. They had no eyes for Pirbright: they looked at Jack with mystified awe.

'Did you land the plane?' asked Fordyce.

Jack blinked. It hadn't occurred to him till that moment.

'Yes,' he said. 'Yes, I did.'

'It was perfect,' said Spinks and looked down at Pirbright. Then he looked at Jack and said, with real admiration, 'He owes you a lot.'

A jeep was speeding across the grass and pulled up with a squeal. O'Brian jumped out, furious.

'All right, who was in that plane?'

'Sergeant Pirbright and Cadet Rayner, sir,' said Fordyce.

'What the hell's the matter with Pirbright?' O'Brian demanded.

'He needs a doctor,' said Jack. 'He had a fit in the air.'

O'Brian stared at him.

'Did you land the plane by yourself?'

'Yes, sir,' said Jack.

'Well, blow me down,' said O'Brian. 'I'd better send for the MO.'

He looked at the driver of the jeep.

'On your way, corporal,' he said.

The jeep roared off over the grass. Soon an RAF ambulance appeared in the distance, growing larger every second. O'Brian said, 'There'll be hell to pay over this, for me as well as you.'

He stood thinking, kicking a little hole in the ground with the toecap of his shoe. Jack remembered he'd done just the same after the crash.

Then he looked up and said, 'Ah well, there's one thing certain. Cadet Sergeant Pirbright won't ever be flying a Spitfire, or anything else for that matter. I wouldn't like to be the one to break the news to him.'

'Perhaps his brother could,' muttered Ronnie Peabody.

'By the way, Rayner, that was well done,'

said O'Brian. 'You looked a real natural.'

Even though he'd been praised, Jack didn't feel too good about it. Pirbright might be a conceited rat but he didn't deserve to have the great ambition that he'd set his heart on wrenched away from him like this.

Flying Officer O'Brian seemed to know what he was thinking. 'The RAF's bigger than any of us, Rayner,' he said. 'And the war's even bigger. You've got to be in perfect shape to fly those monsters in the sky and friend Pirbright will have to come to terms with the fact that he's not.'

He scuffed his toecap in the grass yet again and then looked up smiling. 'But do you know what?'

'No, sir?' said Jack. It came out like a question.

'I reckon you would be,' said O'Brian.

Look out for these other great titles in the *Shades* series:

Animal Lab
by Malcolm Rose

Jamie hates the fact he's gone bald. But can it be right that the animal lab where he works is using monkeys to find a cure?

Mind's Eye
by Gillian Philip

Braindeads like Conor are scary. Or that's what Lara used to think....

Four Degrees More

by Malcolm Rose

When Leyton Curry see
his house fall into the sea,
there's nothing he can
do...
Or is there?

Hauntings

by Mary Chapman

Rebecca Jane opens her
birthday presents and
walks into a living
nighmare, because a
ghostly presence appears
to be taking over her
life...

Cuts Deep
by Catherine Johnson

Devon's heading for
trouble till he meets
Savannah, and starts to
change. But can he ever
put the past behind him?

Virus
by Mary Chapman

Penna's life is
controlled by a computer
programme. Until a
virus gets into the system
and the whole world is
under threat…

Man Trap
by Tish Farrell

Danny doesn't want to be a hunter, but the rains have failed and he and his father must go out poaching or his family will starve. Then Danny makes a fatal mistake…

Danger Money
by Mary Chapman

Bob Thompson is thrilled when he goes to work on the Admiral, an armed smack defending itself against German U boats. But it's not long before he really has to earn his danger money…